Anonymous

Our Merchant Marine

Its condition as shown

Anonymous

Our Merchant Marine
Its condition as shown

ISBN/EAN: 9783337419073

Printed in Europe, USA, Canada, Australia, Japan

Cover: Foto ©Andreas Hilbeck / pixelio.de

More available books at **www.hansebooks.com**

OUR MERCHANT MARINE

ITS CONDITION AS SHOWN BY

THE ADMINISTRATION

AND

THE ADMIRAL OF THE NAVY

✤1888✤

ISSUED BY THE

AMERICAN SHIPPING AND INDUSTRIAL LEAGUE

FOREIGN CARRYING TRADE.

FROM THE REPORT OF HON. C. S. FAIRCHILD
SECRETARY OF THE TREASURY.

The following table shows the values of the imports and exports of the United States carried respectively in American vessels and in foreign vessels during each fiscal year, from 1856 to 1887, inclusive, with the percentage carried in American vessels.

Year ending June 30.	In American vessels.	In foreign vessels.	Total.	Percent'ge carried in American vessels.
1856.........	$482,268,274	$159,336,576	$641,604,850	75.2
1857.........	510 331,027	213,519,796	723,850,823	70.5
1858...... .	447,191,304	160,066,267	607,257,571	73.7
1859.........	465,741 881	229,816,211	695,557,592	66.9
1860.........	507,247,757	255,040,798	762,288,550	66.5
1861.........	381,516,788	203,478,278	584,995,066	65.2
1862.........	217,695,418	218,015,296	435,710,714	50.0
1863.........	241,872,471	343,056,031	584,928,502	41.4
1864...	184,061,486	485,793 518	669,855 034	27.5
1865.........	167,402,872	437,010,124	604,412,996	27.7
1866.........	325,711,861	685 226 691	1,010 928,552	32 2
1867.........	297,834,904	581,330,403	879,165,307	33.9
1868.........	297,981,573	550,546,074	848,527 647	35 1
1869...... ..	289,956,772	586,492,012	876,448,784	33.1
1870.........	352,969,401	638,927,488	991,896,889	35.6
1871.........	353,664,172	755,822,576	1,132,472,258	31.2
1872........	345,331,101	839,346 362	1,212,328 233	28.5
1873........	346,806,592	966,723,651	1,340,800,221	25 8
1874........	350,451,994	939,206,106	1,312,680,640	26.7
1875........	314,257,792	884,788,517	1,219,434,544	25 8
1876.	311,076,171	813 354,987	1,142,904,312	33 1
1877........	316,060,281	859,920,536	1,194,045 637	26 5
1878........	313,050,906	876,991,129	1,210,519,399	25.9
1879........	272,015,692	911,269,232	1,202,708,609	22.6
1880........	258,340,577	1,224,265,434	1,503,503,404	17.18
1881.......	250,586,420	1,289,002,983	1,545,041,974	16.22
1882...... ..	227,229,745	1,212,978,760	1,475,181,831	15 40
1883........	240,420,500	1,258,506,024	1,547,020,316	15.54
1884........	233,699,085	1,127,795,199	1,408,211,302	16.60
1885....... .	194,865,743	1,079 518,566	1,319,717,084	14.76
1886........	197,349,503	1,073,011,118	1,314,960,966	15.01
1887........	194,356,746	1,165,194,508	1,408,502,979	13.80

Thus it will be seen that our foreign commerce, carried in vessels of the United States, measured by its value, has steadily declined from 75 per cent. in 1856 to less than 14 per cent. in 1887. Even of this small percentage less than one-half was carried in steam vessels bearing our flag.

THE NAVAL RESERVE.

FROM THE REPORT OF HON. W. C. WHITNEY,
SECRETARY OF THE NAVY.

The policy of this country has always been opposed to the establishment of large permanent naval and military organizations. This policy, for a country with a great coast line and important commercial interests, almost necessitates the maintenance of auxiliaries in the way of naval and military reserves. The land forces have such auxiliaries in the shape of State militia or national guards. These constitute large bodies of troops, well organized and equipped, thoroughly well trained and disciplined, ready to take the field and to become a part of a regular military estabishment when required.

A public feeling seems to exist for the creation of a naval reserve.

Committees of the Chambers of Commerce of New York and San Francisco have passed resolutions urging the organization of such a force as a means for providing for the coast defence and meeting the increased demands of the regular naval establishment for men and vessels upon the outbreak of war. Inquiries have also been made at the Department from cities of the Great Lakes, and meetings have been held in cities of the South indorsing the formation of such a national organization.

The Department has informed itself fully of the different systems of organization for coast defence and naval reserves at present in force

in foreign countries, and is prepared to formu-
late a general plan for a similar organization to
meet the requirements and conditions of our
own institutions. It should resemble in organization that of the militia or national guard, rest
upon the foundation of local interest, contemplate the employment and rapid mobilization of
steamers enrolled on an auxiliary navy list, and
be calculated to produce the best results upon a
comparatively small national expenditure. I
ask for this question the earnest consideration
of Congress.

It may not be out of place as a branch of this
subject to call attention to one of the incidental
consequences of the policy pursued by other
countries in this matter of a naval reserve. In
time of war troop ships or transports are in
great demand. Several European Governments
make an annual contribution, based on tonnage,
to companies constructing new vessels. The
consideration to the Government is a counter
agreement, permitting the Government to take
such a vessel for a transport in time of war
upon terms named in the agreement. The
Government officials are also consulted as to
her mode of construction, and she goes on to
the naval reserve list. These payments are inci-
dentally in the nature of a subsidy to the ship
owner and this, with the liberal payments for
Government transportation of mails, etc., keeps
a large fleet of merchantmen afloat as a reserve
ready for a time of war. Without ships and
trained seamen there can be no naval reserve.

A notable illustration of the generosity and
courage with which England pushes her shipping interest is seen in the manner in which she
is at this moment dealing with the trade of the

North Pacific. It has been thus far principally
under the American flag and contributory to San
Francisco and the United States. The British
Government and Canada together are proposing
for the establishment of a line of first-class
steamers from Vancouver to Japan. The subsidy
is likely to be $300,000 annually—£45,000 from
England and £15,000 from Canada. There will
also be contributed from the naval reserve fund
probably $5 per ton annually for each ship con-
structed for the route, which will increase the
sum by probably $125,000. Under such com-
petition it is quite easy to conjecture what will
become of the American flag and our resources
in the way of a naval reserve in the North
Pacific.

OUR MERCHANT MARINE.

FROM THE REPORT OF ADMIRAL D. D. PORTER,
UNITED STATES NAVY.

I.

At present there is a great desire in this country to share with others in the foreign trade, and it is strongly urged that the Government should give its aid in resurrecting our ocean commercial marine, since it is very evident that our shipping cannot be revived without the same assistance that was given the ocean steam lines of Great Britain, France, Italy, Germany and latterly, Spain. Heretofore, when it has been proposed in Congress to grant Government aid to assist in putting afloat lines of ocean steamers, questions of free trade and tariff have been introduced to kill the measure, and foreigners who do not wish any competition with their lucrative business, and have plenty of money with which to operate, are always ready to show how much more advantageous it is to Americans that they should have the carrying trade. Foreigners generally argue that they receive no "subsidies," but who knows but themselves what assistance they receive from their Governments?

They carry the United States mails at a low figure to keep American vessels from being built to carry them. It costs them little or nothing to carry the mails and they can well spare the small amount of room required. That lines of American steamers should carry the mails is doubtless the desire of every American, and the feeling on this subject is increasing all over the country. At the same time every merchant knows that a line of American ocean steamships cannot be maintained without subsidies from the Government. In regard to this a misapprehension prevails among the uninformed, who consider it a proposition for the Government to "foster monopolies."

Now, there is a great difference between granting a subsidy and fostering a monopoly. In the latter case, the sole power and permission to deal with a certain place or in a certain article is granted, while the case of a subsidy is simply an assistance to an enterprise from which a return is expected, and such subsidies as I have advocated should not be confined to any particular line of steamers, but should be given to all shipowners who are willing to make their ships conform, in a prescribed degree, to the requirements of a vessel of war, said ships to be constructed under the supervision of the Secretary of the Navy.

This is what other commercial nations do, and it is only justice to the Navy and the country that we should pursue a course that will double or treble the number of our cruisers in time of war. One way of granting a subsidy would be to enact the "tonnage bill" several times brought before Congress. This bill provides that 30 cents per ton shall be allowed every vessel propelled by sail or steam and built and owned in the United States and trading with foreign countries, for every thousand miles sailed or steamed, the contract to hold good for a term of years, with such restrictions regarding the vessels as the Government shall impose,

This would be the simplest plan for resurrecting the mercantile marine and the Government would have at its disposal a class of vessels little inferior to the regular cruising ships of war. In fact, the chances are the steam merchant vessels would be superior in speed, which should be the chief desideratum with commerce destroyers. By a proper subsidy, such as I have indicated, many industries would be assisted, those of iron and steel, coal mining, shipyards, canvas, boat-building, hardware, glass-making, pottery, furniture, painters, engine-builders; in short, a hundred different branches of trade which combine to make a complete vessel, industries that are now languishing for want of this very stimulus which they would enjoy but for the lack of forethought in those who should labor to advance every employment in which our citizens are engaged.

It is not so much the building proper of American steamships that makes them cost more than vessels constructed abroad, as it is the expense of fitting them out; for there is not sufficient competition in this country to bring that kind of work down to the standard of foreign countries where labor is so much cheaper. Ships built in Great Britain cost ten per cent. less; but, when the better finish of American ships and the superiority of our iron is considered, the statements that it would be better for us to build ships on the Clyde or Mersey are seen to be fallacious.

With all these facts staring our legislators in the face, they should not hesitate a moment between the proposition to abolish the shipping laws so that vessels could be built abroad for us by British mechanics, and that to foster the industries of our own country and have our own ocean steamers constructed in the United States under the supervision of naval officers, so that the Government would have vessels of suitable character to perform the service required of them as commerce destroyers in time of war.

This argument doubtless conflicts with the theories of the free-traders of Great Britain and the United States, who require that England shall do all our carrying trade and reap the profits; but, leaving sentimentality out of the question, we will get better ships built in our own country, although the first cost may be rather more, and we shall have the satisfaction of knowing that the vessels can, if necessary, be used for naval purposes. This is what advocates for increasing our naval resources aim at in supporting the subsidy measure, for we see how little disposition there has been in this country to build up a navy adequate to its wants and dignity; but the officers of the navy hope to see some plan adopted without delay, by which, in the event of war, they can afford the necessary protection to our own commerce and inflict damage on that of the enemy.

There is a growing feeling in the country with regard to the neglect which has been manifested in building up our ocean mercantile marine, and it is to be hoped that this feeling will spread until the thousands of unemployed workmen have a chance to earn good wages and the American ocean steamers have a fair share of the $150,000,000 annually paid to foreigners for carrying our goods.

By the course we have pursued in this country we have actually given protection to foreign steamships at the expense of our own. The wharves of New York are decorated with foreign flags, while hardly an American ensign can be seen floating above a steamer suitable for conversion into a vessel of war. This is free trade with a vengeance, all on one side and for the benefit of other nations. We ship our goods in foreign bottoms and foreigners get the lion's share of the profits. No American steamships are employed in foreign trade, because subsidized ships can drive them off and carry freight cheaper.

It may be denied that these foreign lines are subsidized, but we know they started on a subsidy, which their Government wisely allowed them, and with that aid and the opposition our ship owners met with in this country, owing to a want of liberality on the part of Congress, European steam lines can increase and multiply without opposition from the United States. It does not appear to have occurred to our people how this liberality of foreign nations will react against us some day. These lines of foreign steamships have all the ocean traffic in their hands. They have a perfect right to it, no doubt, as long as they find no one to dispute it. New York, to all appearances, is a foreign port, and owes much of her prosperity to the great ships which steam in and out of the harbor almost as often as the trains run up and down the elevated railroad.

Many of these ocean steamers are grand structures of great speed and strength, and well calculated for commerce destroyers. They could outstrip any cruisers we now have afloat, whatever we may do in the future. Here is a great fleet of steamships built with all the skill of British artisans that could in ten days' time be metamorphosed into vessels of war, armed with heavy guns, ready to blockade our ports and sweep what commerce we have left from the sea, or to encounter our ships in battle. In the ordinary course of events this is not likely to happen, for the interests of Great Britain and the United States are too closely interwoven to make a conflict of arms between them probable, but war has occurred before and may occur again, and I wish particularly to draw attention to a naval power right in our midst, built up and fostered by this country and ready to be used against us. The protection that has been given these foreign lines consists in the repudiation by our legislators of the claims of our own ship owners and failing to grant them assistance to enable them to compete with other nations

I append the names of a few of these great British ships to show what an auxiliary Navy might at this moment have been ours had we taken time by the forelock and devoted our attention to the building up of our own mercantile marine instead of that of foreigners. The list here given includes only a portion of the vessels that can be converted into ships of war, but the fleet would be a powerful one if we could control it.

Name of Ship.	Tons.	Name of Ship.	Tons.
Aurania	7269	Arizona	5147
Bolivia	4050	British Queen	3558
Britannic	5004	City of Richmond	4623
City of Montreal	4480	City of Chicago	5202
City of Rome	8144	Celtic	3867
Devonia	4270	Denmark	3724
England	4898	Etruria	7718
Egypt	4670	Furnessia	5495
Helvetia	4583	Holland	3848
Servia	7302	State of Nebraska	3986
Umbria	7718	Wisconsin	3700
Wyoming	3238		

These facts may be deemed suggestive, and when I mention that the Etruria, one of the above named ships, lately made 496 knots in twenty-four consecutive hours, or over twenty knots an hour, the importance of building similar vessels for our mercantile marine may be estimated. No matter how great a fleet of war vessels a nation may possess, a strong commercial marine is a great addition to it, a matter which is perfectly understood in Europe· Whenever we have been engaged in war our mercantile marine has very greatly contributed to our success. The vessels I have mentioned in the foregoing list form but a small portion of the fleet of clippers which seem at present to have the exclusive right to transport American merchandise across the ocean, and the fact that not a single line of American steamers is employed in transporting material to Europe, is a serious reflection on the enterprise of our citizens and an evidence of neglect on the part of Congress.

II.

As people begin to examine more closely into the subject, the cry of "monopoly" has less weight. Shipping leagues are springing up in all parts of the United States, and the potent arguments advanced at their meetings are sweeping away ·the clouds of prejudice and showing the public the true state of affairs. The word "subsidy," so long a bugbear to our legislators, has begun to lose some of its terrors, and they see in the term "subvention" (a Government aid or bounty) or "postal appropriation" no signs of monopoly in England, while at present we are practically insuring a monopoly in this country to foreign steamship lines.

There is no doubt that the new view of this matter which is taking possession of the American mind has brightened the prospects of our mercantile marine, and it is to be hoped that , the many gloomy years in which our commerce has been at a low ebb may be succeeded by a period of wise legislation in which only a national feeling will prevail. I look for this as hopefully as I do for generous appropriations for the Navy when Congress again assembles.

A closer examination of this subject than has heretofore been given it by the majority of our statesmen will show the loss this country has sustained by a failure of Congress to act in the premises. In the last eight years no less than *one billion two hundred millions of dollars* have been paid to foreign steamships, a sum almost equal to our national debt, and a burden that is only made tolerable owing to the immense resources of our country. We should be still further depleted but for the fact that we are sustained by the tariff on foreign merchandise and the protection of our manufactures, which prevents us from being undersold by foreigners and enables us to give employment to our working people, so that with all our drawbacks we grow rich.

It would be hardly fair to accuse the American people of a want of energy for failing to revive their ocean commerce when they are exhibiting so much of this quality in other directions in developing the resources of the country. It seems to be a law of nature that decadence shall overtake every nation in the course of

time, but there is no instance on record of a
nation giving up her position in the race for
supremacy without a struggle to retrieve herself. The decadence which has afflicted our
ocean carrying trade is not for want of energy
on the part of our people, or for the want of
laws, but perhaps from a plethora of both which
has hampered those who would have labored for
its revival.

This country was not formed by Government,
but was built up by the independent efforts of
a series of individuals who have led the way in
all great enterprises, and in the early days of
the Republic never thought of asking Government aid; but during the great crisis in our
history, when all the men and money of the
country had to be employed to save it from
destruction, the nations of Europe, while we
were hampered with difficulties at home, got so
far ahead of us in the race for commercial supremacy that they have ever since maintained
the lead.

The tendency in this country has not been to
foster and encourage enterprise, but to limit
and destroy it by laws specious enough in read-
ing, but which are like the ashes of Dead Sea
fruit when placed to the lips. To this system
of legislating down hill and closing the door
tightly year after year against the applications
of those who stand ready to enter into the business of reviving the commercial marine, is due
the fact that our ocean carrying trade has
passed into European hands, and that we are
likely to be left with half a dozen machine
shops to help us build a navy in times of war,
or repair the small one on which, in ordinary
times, we seem doomed to rely.

While our present illiberal policy is pursued we stand no chance of ever becoming anything more than a fifth-rate power upon the ocean. If we go on at the present rate our country will lose much of the strength which it owes to the cohesion of its individual atoms, and, like a soul less machine working on at random, it will meet the fate of many other nations that have flourished for a time and then fallen by their own weight.

Laying aside all arguments in favor of a mercantile marine, it is necessary for the assistance of the navy in time of war. We need additional and enlarged markets for our surplus products, but foreign vessels with their subsidies are fast closing all the channels of trade against us, and our manufacturers, who would otherwise help to supply the world, are shut off by British rivals. British steamships have taken possession of all the routes of trade, fostered by the British Government and protected by British guns. This is creditable to the British Government, which looks out for the interests of Englishmen all the world over, and it would seem as if the parent stock of the English-speaking race had more energy than their transatlantic offspring, for their steam mercantile marine not only monopolizes the foreign trade of the United States, but encircles the earth, for there is not a port in the world where there is a chance of finding a market for manufactured articles that a British steamship does not penetrate.

All that is left to us in the way of foreign commerce are the gleanings in the by-ways of trade, about which our great rivals give themselves little concern, and a few second-rate vessels may now and then be encountered trying to make a living under our flag, struggling along like the crows at Pensacola, which have to go to sea to get something to eat. That kind of commerce is of little benefit to a nation. It is necessary to move on the great thoroughfares of the ocean to have an extensive trade, and Great Britain, in recognition of this fact, pays her steam lines liberal subsidies.

As the great highways of ocean trade are not frequented, by American steamships, inquiry ought to be made as to why this is the case and remedies adopted to cure the evil, especially as regards those routes where exports from the United States should naturally be carried in our own vessels, but in 1880, when this country had had ample opportunity to revive her commercial marine, we find the Americans transported goods to the value of $280,000,000, while foreign vessels, mostly steamships, carried $1,309,-466,596, the percentage being in 1856, 75, and in 1880, 17 per cent. This was a tremendous change for a country, and in regard to which a well known statistician observes: "At the beginning of the nineteenth century the commerce of the world seemed to be passing into American hands, American shipping having increased fivefold in twenty years;" yet this once flourishing state of affairs seems to be forgotten by our legislators, which is the more remarkable considering the highly intelligent character of our members of Congress generally.

It was natural to suppose that when this falling off of our commercial marine took place Congress would take advantage of the authority given by the Constitution to regulate commerce with foreign nations, and build it up again. The words of the Constitution are ample warrant to provide that our ships should receive a fair share of the ocean carrying trade, and there is just as much power to regulate our ocean commerce as to regulate commerce between the several States of the Union; but to prevent complications with foreign powers and to avoid laying imposts on foreign vessels that would conflict with treaties, we must give our citizens sufficient subsidies to enable them to build and run lines of steamships equal to any afloat.

What would ten millions a year be to this country if given by Congress to help build up our commercial marine? It would more than return the equivalent in the shape of customs dues. It would more than pay if we could retain in the United States twenty out of the one hundred and fifty millions which are yearly carried out of the country for freights without benefits to our citizens. Why should not American commerce be allowed the same opportunities that are afforded the other industries of the country, which have reached a development such as the most far-seeing never dreamed of? We are not tied down by foreign subsidized competitors on land, and therefore our progress has been marvelous, and so it would be upon the ocean if the bonds were once cut which confine our ship-builders.

We will take, for instance, the French merchant steamships of over 8,000 tons, which of late years have become a feature in transatlantic travel. These vessels were encouraged by their Government as a set-off to the British steamships, which it was seen could be turned into vessels of war at short notice in case of hostilities with France, just as on the late occasion the Russians, when threatened with a war with England, fitted up several large steamers in this country as commerce destroyers. France pays to these steamers $14,000 for every round trip between Havre and New York. What chance could an American line have against such a competition as that, receiving no assist· ance from Government and probably not being paid to carry the mails, which the foreigners would carry for nothing rather than an Ameri can ship should receive aid from the Govern ment? Even giving us "free ships and free materials" would not surmount the difficulty.

Foreigners know this, and do not object to our having fast ships built on the Mersey and the Clyde, as they are aware that we could not run them with any profit, handicapped as we would be by the many advantages possessed by the steamers of Europe. Foreign Governments must have lines of fast ships as offsets to each other in time of war, and are willing to pay for them, but even with Governmental aid the profits of these vessels are not excessive, about six per cent. being the usual limit. Without the subsidy there would be no profit. If there be any lines which do not receive Government aid, it is because they received it until they were able to get along without further assistance. At one time the Cunard Line, with its magnificent fleet, netted 26 per cent. If this line should, for any cause, fail to pay a fair dividend, it will be for the interest of Great Britain to subsidiz it again.

After all, the amount required to subsidize a line of steamers is not so very great. Suppose the United States started to subsidize forty ocean steamers the size of those that cross the Atlantic. Putting the vessels at 8,000 tons each, and allowing 30 cents per ton for every 1,000 miles traveled, the expense would be $2,400 per 1,000 miles for the 3,000 miles, or $7,200 for the voyage, return trip the same, or $14,400 for the round trip. Assuming eight round trips a year would give $115,200 annually for each steamer, or for the whole forty vessels $4,608,000 for a grand fleet of ships worthy of this Republic, any two of which would be worth more in time of war than all the cruisers we have at present in the Navy.

Yet $4,500,000 is no great amount for a nation to pay that has so many millions locked up in her Treasury doing no good, while every legitimate opportunity should be taken to enlarge the avenues of trade by land and sea in order that our country may fulfill the grand destiny marked out for it.

Besides my interest as a citizen in the advancement of the country, I am specially concerned in behalf of the Navy, and am endeavoring to show for how small a sum an auxiliary naval force can be maintained. We spend more than the amount I have mentioned in public buildings, and treble the sum in river and harbor improvements, and I would inquire which of these three appropriations would be of the greatest benefit to the country, to say nothing of the more important part we would play in foreign countries? In time of war this great adjunct to our Navy would commit havoc on the enemy's commerce all over the world, while the heavy ships were defending our coasts. This is a grand picture to contemplate, but I fear a delusive one. Judging from the past, we are not equal to the occasion.

III.

Notwithstanding our former experience, we seem to have learned nothing, and, as regards our commercial marine, are actually in a worse condition than we were in 1812. Speaking interestedly, I look at the loss to the Navy through the lack of energetic action on the part of our people and of unwise legislation on the part of Congress. I refer to the want of means to properly man a great fleet in time of war, which, under present circumstances, would be impossible, no matter how many naval ships we might build. A navy cannot be improvised or built at short notice, a fact which all history demonstrates, but it requires some strong incentive to build it up, such as a powerful enemy near at hand, a commerce to protect, or injuries to avenge, and those nations that have dominated the world for so many years have attained their naval greatness only through a long course of training and learning how to turn to account every possible factor in the event of war. After a long series of hostilities between Great Britain and France, the conviction was forced upon the latter nation that the only way to compete with her rival was to build a navy of equal force. When this scheme was proposed in the French Assembly Mirabeau remarked:

"The English war marine has grown to what it is, like the English oaks, of which the ships are built, through the slow progress of a thousand years. You cannot have a navy without sailors, and sailors are made through the dangers of the deep, from father to son, until their home is on the wave. You cannot build up a navy at once by a simple act of legislation."

These memorable words are as true to-day as they were when uttered.

We must not expect to go on from year to year neglecting everything that tends to increase the naval strength of our country and then by some spasm of legislation create at once a navy or mercantile marine. In the case of a mercantile marine there will have to be overcome the opposing elements that have stood for years in the way of a great industry, and the first step should therefore be to appropriate money liberally, for money is the Archimedean lever that moves the world. No meagre aid should be doled out to repair the mischief created by unwise economy in the past, but such assistance should be given as will infuse life into every part of the Republic and give employment to hundreds of thousands who to-day are without encouragement to ply their trades, a body of mechanics of whom the country may be proud, and upon whom the Government must rely in time of war.

It is the interest of a commercial nation to have as great a balance of trade in its favor as possible. Great Britain, with this idea in view, is constantly increasing her tonnage, and endeavors to have all her imports and exports carried in her own vessels, thus realizing nearly the entire selling price of her exports in foreign markets, and for her imports pays only the selling price in those same markets. If we had our own vessels, with which to carry on our trade, most of the freight charges would be retained or returned to this country, whereas $150,000,000 are annually retained or returned to England. With many people this is a mere matter of "sentiment." They do not care how it is done so that they get their goods to a market, utterly ignoring the question of patriotism which should ever animate the hearts of Americans. But even in the breast of the most callous there must occasionally be a feeling of regret at the thought of our flag disappearing from the ocean, like a meteor that flashed for a moment over the surface of the waters and then disappeared forever.

But yet there is hope. We are still the young giant among nations, whose muscles are temporarily relaxed, and the time may yet come when the American mind, grasping the situation of affairs, will exert its powers to place upon the ocean a fleet of steamers that will be the pride of the nation, and will inaugurate a new era more striking than any previous event in our commercial history.

Many persons who cannot be moved by argument or touched by an appeal to their patriotic sensibilities can be convinced by an array of statistics which will show the country is suffering, and how we are handicapped by foreign nations. Not only our traditional commercial rival, Great Britain, but the other nations of Europe have taken the lead of us on the ocean. It is no longer said, " All the foreign commerce of the world is passing into American hands," but "All American ocean commerce is passing into the hands of foreigners." These are facts easily substantiated.

In the first place, I propose to show that the great ocean steam marine of Great Britain owes its existence solely to subsidies, although many efforts have been made to prove the contrary. Parliamentary papers prove that the system is more than a century old, which shows that

British statesmen were wiser in days of old than we are at present, notwithstanding the example we have had before us. Great Britain started with the idea of building up her industries on a basis that would eclipse all other countries, and her ocean marine was so essential a part of British greatness that from the first it received the most particular attention. The following taken from the reports of the " American Shipping and Industrial League," will show how much British commerce owes to subsidies (see 22d British Report of Commission of Revenue Inquiry), viz:

The attention of the commissioners of " fees and gratuities," in the year 1788, was drawn to the expenditure, which had been increased in the packet service during several years preceding their inquiry, an expenditure, according to their expression, " so enormous as almost to surpass credibility," the sum of $5,200,000, giving an annual expenditure (in a period of seventeen years) the sum of $305,000.

Here is official British investigation and evidence of shipping subsidy by England, viz.:

1770 to 1788..	$5,200,000
This continued until next examination by committee of finance, 1797, which shows that instead of being stopped it was increased, averaging up to 1810 $302,200 yearly, or in all, 1788 to 1810.........	8,628,200
The committee (1810) also increased the subsidy to $525,000 per year, and continued increasing until 1816, making a total of...................	4,725,000
After which it fell of for three years, 1817 to 1820, to	1,655,000
The spirit of subsidy again arose from 1821 to 1830, and paid...	5,855,000
Making in the first sixty years a payment of....	$25,063,000

It was at this time (1830) that the British commissioner of revenue made an especial investigation " for the purpose of inquiring into collection and management of public revenue," and then began the heavy subsidizing of steamships to over $500,000 per annum, as follows, viz.:

1830 to 1837.............................	$6,000,000
From general post-office, 1837 to 1849............	25,000,000
From mercantile marine fund, 1823 to 1848.........	37,500,000
From general post-office:	
1850 to 1859 (over)........................	60,000,000
1860 to 1869...............................	50,000,000
1870 to 1885..............................	70,000,000

Total assistance from British treasury to her shipping. $273,563,000

This does not include "amounts especially authorized" by Parliament from time to time, or added from "mercantile marine fund," or amounts made up by the British system of "averaging and adjusting the accounts of her mail steamship companies," in order to enable them to declare an annual dividend of at least eight per cent.

In order to anticipate the plea that such was the case, but that England does not now subsidize, the following is taken from official publications:

BRITISH MAIL SUBSIDY.

[Report of the British Postmaster-General, 1885.]

Line of Packets	Contracts		Payment.
	Commencement	Termination.	
Australia:			
Point de Galle and Melbourne, Singapore and Brisbane, San Francisco and Sidney.	Contracts with	colonial governments	£4,888
Brazil, River Plate and Chili:			
Bi-monthly from Southampton	Sept. 1, 1876	On six months' notice.	8,870
Fortnightly service from Liverpool	July 1, 1878	On six months' notice.	2,774
Cape of Good Hope and Natal	Contracts with	colonial governments	5,218
Cyprus and Alexandria			
East Indies, China and Japan	Feb. 1, 1880	Six months' notice.	360,000
Europe:			
Dover and Calais			12,034
Dover and Ostend			4,500
Malta, etc.			640
North America:			
United States	Dec. 1, 1877	On six months' notice.	96,590
Halifax, Bermuda and Saint Thomas	Jan. 1, 1878.	On twelve months' notice	17,500
Pacific	July 1, 1878.	On six months' notice.	8,418
West Indies:			
Bi-monthly service	Jan. 1, 1880.	On Dec. 31, 1885.	80,500
Non-contract service			415
Additional Service:			
Liverpool and Puerto Cabello, Tampico and Santa Martha	Oct. 1, 1881.	On six months' notice.	764
Balize annd New Orleans	Contract with minating September 30, 1889.	Honduras Governm't ter-	1,800
Turk's Island and Saint Thomas	Contract with Turk's Island Governm't.		300
West coast of Africa	No contract.		9,082
Total			668,788

Detailed statement from "financial account" shows £774,626, or $3,870,000.

By reference to Secretary Evarts' letter (Com. Rel., 1879, p. 26) the detailed "table of trade of West Indies" shows that only one-half of Great Britian's trade is with her own possessions, hence one-half of her subsidy can b credited to the benefit of her colonies. * * *

This settles the subsidy or subvention matter, or whatever name we may choose to call it, and should close the door against the schemes of foreign agents who are plotting to keep lines of American steamships from showing themselves on the ocean so that we may confine our shipping to the small vessels that creep along our coast. One would think that any American with proper pride of country would burn with indignation at the idea of our playing such an insignificant part—a game in which we may get the shell while our rivals secure the oyster. Consider for a moment the result of our submitting so long to this iron rule which affects every industry in the United States.

IV.

The number of steam vessels in the world is given in the following table, which is taken from the Repertore Général of the Bureau Veritas published during the present year, and includes all steamers of whatever class above 100 tons burden:

Flag.	Num-ber.	Gross Tons.	Flag.	Num-ber.	Gross Tons.
British.........	4,906	6,545,645	Argentine......	22	13,120
French.........	468	745,660	Chinese........	9	11,832
German........	529	601,975	Turkish........	17	11,770
American......	879	506,668	Hawaiian	12	10,127
Spanish.	856	399,577	Peruvian.......	5	5,951
Dutch..........	167	210,549	Haytien........	4	4,087
Italian.....	158	204,058	Zanzibar.......	2	2,823
Russian........	218	165,447	Uruguay	4	2,396
Norwegian......	275	147,011	Roumanian	8	2,125
Swedish........	329	137,377	Tunisian.......	2	1,762
Austrian.	105	135,145	Honduras......	1	989
Danish.........	174	127,830	Persian	1	835
Belgian.........	62	111,746	Venezuelan	8	638
Japanese.......	101	92,479	Costa Rican....	2	719
Greek	57	54,614	Siamese........	2	547
Brazilian.......	82	49,216	Ecuador.	1	829
Egyptian.......	28	22,674	San Domingo ..	1	167
Portuguese.....	27	26,515			
Chilian....	23	24,925	Total....	8,547	10,403,958
Mexican.	12	18,456			

This statement shows at a glance the sorry figure which our country cut in the enrollment, and it must be remembered that of the 379 steamers with which the United States are credited (which includes tugs, river boats and old, obsolete craft of all sorts), but 101 are actually fitted to navigate the open ocean, and only 15 can be properly classed as ocean-sailing steamers. This last class are those running from New York to Aspinwall and Brazil, and from San Francisco to Panama, Australia, and China and Japan. All the others are coastwise vessels.

I give below a list of American steamers which make up the 101 vessels referred to above. In compiling it I have rejected all vessels built previous to 1865, all wooden and paddle steamers and all below 1,000 tons.

LIST OF IRON AND STEEL STEAMERS OF OVER 3,000 TONS.

When built.	Name.	Tons	When built.	Name.	Tons
1883..	Alameda............	3,158	1875..	City of New York ..	3,019
1878.	City of Para.........	3,532	1874..	City of Peking......	5,079
1878..	City of Rio deJaneiro	3,548	1875..	City of Syducy......	3,016
1884..	El Dorado...........	3,531	1884..	El Paso.............	3,531
1884..	Eureka	3,531	1862..	Excelsior...........	3,264
1873..	Illinois.............	3,101	1873..	Indiana	3,101
1883..	Mariposa............	3,158	1873..	Ohio......	3,101
1872..	Pennsylvania........	3,104	1883..	San Pablo..........	3,119
1882..	San Pedro.	3,119			

Total, 17 steamers, 57,012 tons. Other nations have 484 steamers of over 3,000 tons.

BETWEEN 2,000 AND 3,000 TONS.

When built.	Name.	Tons	When built.	Name.	Tons
1873..	Acapulco...........	2,572	1883..	Advance	2,604
1883..	Alamo.............	2,943	1876..	Algiers.........	2,287
1881..	Alleghany...........	2,014	1881..	Berkshire...........	2,014
1879..	Chalmette.	2,983	1884..	Chatham	2,72X
1882..	Chattahoochee	2,676	1883..	Cienfuegos...	2,832
1879..	City of Alexandria..	2,480	1880..	City of Augusta......	2,870
1877..	City of Macon.......	2,093	1882..	City of Puebla.	2,841
1877..	City of Savannah....	2,029	1877..	City of Washington .	2,618
1870..	Clyde..............	2,017	1873..	Colima.............	2,906
1879..	Colorado............	2,765	1873..	Colon	2,691
1880..	Columbia...........	2,722	1885..	Comal	2,934
1879..	Decatur II. Miller...	2,296	1883..	Finance	2,603
1873..	Grenada	2,572	1882..	Guyandotte	2,351
1884..	H. F. Dimmock.....	2,626	1883..	Lampasas............	2,943
1875..	Lone Star...........	2,255	1880..	Louisiana	3,000
1876..	Morgan City........	2,217	1883..	Nacoochee	2,689
1875..	New York...........	2,284	1880..	Newport............	2,735
1877..	Niagara	2,265		Onoka (lake steamer)	2,100
1878..	Oregon........	2,385	1885..	Philadelphia.......	2,099
1882..	Queen of the Pacific	2,728	1876..	Rio Grande..........	2,566
1882..	Roanoke	2,354	1882..	San Blas	2,075
1882..	San Jose	2,081	1882..	San Juan............	2,076
1881..	San Marcos....	2,839	1884..	Santa Rosa..........	2,417
1879..	Santiago.............	2,359	1878	Saratoga	2,426
1884..	Seneca	2,729	1881..	Starbuck	2,157
1878..	State of California...	2,266	1882..	Tallahassee..........	2,660
	Tioga (lake steamer).	2,000	1881..	Umatilla	2,131
1881..	Walla Walla.........	2,135	1881..	Willamette	2,562

Total, 56 steamers, 138,155 tons. Other nations have 1,819 steamers of from 2,000 to 3,000 tons.

BETWEEN 1,000 AND 2,000 TONS.

When built.	Name.	Tons.	When built.	Name.	Tons
1877..	Aransas'.....	1,157	1880..	Breakwater........	1,045
1881..	Caracas	1,589	1884..	City of Topeka	1,057
1872..	City of San Antonio	1,605	1875..	City of Atlanta	1,621
1880..	City of Columbia ..	1,878	1874..	City of Chester ...	1,106
1874..	City of Panama....	1,490	1868..	Costa Rica.........	1,457
1870..	Georgia...........	1,900	1878..	Gate City........	1,993
1878..	General Whitney...	1,848	1873..	George W. Elder...	1,709
1872..	George W. Clyde...	1,805	1866..	Harlan......	1,163
1873..	Johns Hopkins'....	1,471	1873..	Knickerbocker	1,642
1879..	Manhattan	1,525	1872..	New Orleans......	1,440
1881..	Ozama	1,028	1873..	Richmond....	1,435
1873..	State of Texas.....	1,549	1833..	Spartan...........	1,599
1883..	Valencia......... .	1,598	1871..	William Crane	1,417
1869..	William Lawrence .	1,047	1877..	Yaquina....	1,241

Total, 28 steamers, 41,415 tons. Other nations have over 2,600 steamers of from 1,000 to 2,000 tons.

RECAPITULATION.

Class.	No	Tons.
Steamers over 8,000 tons................................	17	57,012
Steamers between 2,000 and 8,000 tons...............	56	138,155
Steamers between 1,000 and 2,000 tons...............	28	41,415
Grand total...............	101	236,585

This is a very poor exhibit of American sea-going steamers. It shows very few above 3,000 tons, and not all of these are employed. A line of steamships was started from Philadelphia to Europe, consisting of the Illinois, Indiana, Ohio and Pennsylvania, each of 3,100 tons, but it was soon found that they could not compete with foreign lines for causes already stated. Then they were purchased by the Pennsylvania

Railroad Company and started out again on a quixotic career. The same result followed, and the company had to withdraw and lay them up —a long row of hulks now, looking very much like those of the Navy laid up in "Rotten Row." Their short existence indicated that the national spirit which influenced a portion of our citizens met with no corresponding feeling in other quarters, and these vessels became the victims of that temerity which now and then animate citizens anxious to redeem our commerce and place the flag once more upon the sea.

The above tables show what an increase there has been in foreign tonnage, owing to the system of subsidies. In addition to this, in 1860, ships built of iron were gaining in popular favor abroad, an idea that was encouraged in England because ships could be built of a ma terial of which England had an abundance, whereas her supply of timber was limited. In the mean time, the United States, with plenty of timber, but building no iron ships, began to feel the effects of the new mode of construction in Great Britian, and in consequence were compelled to accept low rates of freight, and, at length, to sell their ships, so that in 1865 we had but one-third of our foreign commerce, while that of Great Britian had largely in-creased.

The iron ships were encouraged by the British Government, for it was seen what a preponderance in tonnage would soon be given their mercantile marine, while the United States did nothing to encourage shipbuilding, except forbidding registers to foreign-built vessels, and no plant existed in the country for turning out such ships as were being multiplied in Great Britian. It would seem as if our countrymen were so bewildered by the number and size of the steamers constructed abroad, and so delighted at the luxurious accommodation afforded European travelers at so reasonable a rate, that they became converts to the English idea, forgetting that the advent of these steamers was a death-blow to the hope of reviving our ocean steam marine.

Since that time the decline of our vessels has continued, and at present the tonnage of this country engaged in foreign trade is less than it was in 1810, and if no remedy is applied, it will ere long disappear from the ocean. The advocates of free ships contend that the existing state of affairs is largely owing to our navigation laws, and that the only remedy is to authorize the building of our vessels on the Clyde and Mersey; but I think it safe to say that the repeal of our navigation laws would result in the destruction of our coastwise carrying trade, and that the art of shipbuilding would be one of the lost arts as far as we are concerned. The best argument against this plan is that the nation which has so nearly succeeded in driving us from the ocean is a strong advocate for free ships.

Our present facilities for building iron and steel ships are poor enough, as is shown by the fact that none of the builders could contract at once for the ships lately authorized by Congress and agree to finish them in a stated time, while in England such contracts would be accepted in a week, and the ships would be in commission in eighteen months. From this circumstance arises the desire of many people to have our ships built abroad instead of devoting their energies to increasing the facilities at home, when the same results would follow here as now obtain in Great Britain.

But suppose we could purchase a ship in England for $600,000 that would cost $700,000 in this country. Would it be any profit to the United States that the purchaser gained $100,000 while the nation lost $600,000 spent in foreign labor and material? Would it not be better to retain the money at home and circulate it among our mechanics and laborers? In such matters we might well take a leaf from England's book. She spares no effort to keep her laboring people employed in building up her great commercial marine and invincible navy.

I remember when American merchants were the most prominent men all along the Pacific coast of this continent, and our flag, waving at the peak of our splendid ships, outnumbered all others four to one. Americans held nearly all the trade, and then it was foreigners cried out that it was all passing into our hands. But to-day how great the difference! There are no American merchants to speak of; they have handed over all their right and title to trade to the British merchants, to whom are consigned the numerous steamships loaded with goods, among which none from our country will be found. England has captured our trade, and we are now, like the little fish that follow in the wake of the shark, gaining a scanty subsistence from the monster's leavings.

V.

EAST INDIA TRADE.

It has been the ambition of the leading commercial nations for centuries to control the trade with the East Indies. The nation that could do it would dominate the commercial world.

In the palmy days of our commerce, when our great clipper ships made such quick passages from China and India to England and the United States, there seemed a fair prospect of the bulk of the trade falling into American hands, but the building of great ocean steamships and the granting of generous subsidies by the British Government put a stop to all this. America, with the best of iron and the best of mechanical skill, could not compete with her rival. Trip-hammers do not grow spontaneously, and a plant such as was established in England can only be provided by great capitalists backed by the aid of Government.

Driven from the ocean, we tried what could be done on land, and by Government assistance built the railroads to the Pacific, part of the straight and short road to India, China and Japan. The project then was to subsidize a line of steamers from San Francisco to China and Japan, and the great trade with those countries would be ours; the time from New York to Hong-Kong would be thirty-four days, whereas by the old route around the cape of Good Hope eighty-six days were required, with all the vicissitudes of weather and climate. We subsidized a line of steamers, which was eminently successful as long as the subsidy lasted, but at length the British put steamships on this route, which curtailed the American profits very materially, and the stoppage of the subsidy to the Pacific Mail Steamship Company reduced its line to an ordinary affair, and our promised wealth flowed into British coffers.

Thus the hopes of American trade with Japan

particularly, turned out delusive, and the matter stands about as follows:

FOREIGN COMMERCE OF JAPAN.

Country.	Imports.	Exports.	Total.
Great Britain...............	$15,878,000	$ 3,084,000	$18,962,000
United States..............	1,533,000	10,854,000	12,387,000
France....................	3,128,000	7,048,000	10,176,000

So with the short, straight route to Japan, we lost the race, and when the Pacific Mail Steamship Company's line runs down for want of subsidies, all the carrying trade will pass into British hands.

The imports of China and Hong-Kong, together with all other Asiatic countries, amounted, in 1879, to $754,669,000, of which amount Great Britian had $281,631,000, France, $22,893,-000, and the United States, $17,510,000. The exports were $772,766,000; to Great Britian, $225,-806,000, and to the United States, $53,838,000, showing that in the China trade the Americans fared no better than in the trade with Japan, notwithstanding our straight line to the Indies, all of which is because the English have a system which enables them to secure the greatest portion of the ocean carrying trade, while we have no system whatever.

England is now beating us with our own weapons. The Canadian Pacific Railroad will soon be in complete operation, and Canada has paid this tribute to England, not perhaps with the idea of diverting all the trade through the Dominion, but with the hope of obtaining a large share of it. Canada offers to pay $75,000 a year to a line of steamers between Vancouver's

Island and Hong Kong to connect with the railway, and $125,000 a year to an Australian line on condition that the British Government pay $225,000 yearly to the former line. Should this arrangement be effected, the Canadian Pacific Railroad Company's purposes will be aided by an annual grant of $425,000, at 3 per cent., the equivalent of a cash subsidy of $14,-000,000. Great Britian's contribution will secure her a military route well worth the money.

Thus Great Britain, either to secure the trade of a country or a military route to her possessions, merely applies the subsidy touchstone to all corporations that tend to strengthen the Empire. This line at once becomes a powerful competitor with the American lines, which will soon go to the wall unless proper support is given them. The Canadian Pacific Railroad is not likely to yield in itself any profits for many years, but it will put a stopper on American lines of steamships in the Pacific, and so far cripple our naval resources in that quarter.

By the simple process of paying a small subsidy, Great Britain controls a line of railroad across the continent, maintains a strong military and naval depot at Vancouver Island, and runs a line of steamers to China and Japan, which will enable thousands of the Chinese coolies, who have struck such terror into the inhabitants of our Pacific States, to invade our country from the North. We have held the subsidy business to be of no account, but it has done wonders for the British mercantile marine, and I see no reason why it should not do the same for that of the United States.

The British system of keeping up her lines

of ocean steamers is never lost sight of nor neglected. It is as carefully looked after as her navy, for the navy could not get along in case of a great war without the aid of the merchant steamers. In looking back at the marine history of England, it is noticeable that the decade embraced between the years 1840 and 1850 effected a revolution in the affairs of her ocean commerce. At that epoch fears were entertained that the commerce of Great Britain was on the decline, owing principally to the rapid growth of the United States as a maritime power. Mr. Cunard, who had built the first four steamships to run from England to America, under an annual Government subsidy of $400,000, was enabled to have his compensation increased to $560,000, or more than 50 per cent. of the cost of the four steamers. Six years later, when two new vessels were added to the line, the subsidy was increased to $700,000, and was continued for fifteen years. The Peninsular and Oriental Steamship Company received subsidies to the extent of $1,000,000, and the Royal Mail Steamship Company was established by the same means, which made these lines such a financial success that the fears of Great Britain losing her ocean supremacy were allayed and a turning point noted in the history of her commercial marine.

Since that period the attention of the British Government has been constantly applied to the extension of their steam tonnage—so much so that the business of building steamers was rather overdone, and finally there were at least 1,000,000 tons more than could be profitably used. This superfluity was the origin of the great clamor that broke out a few years ago in

favor of "free ships." The British hoped to
sell us their surplus vessels, and the free traders
of this country were in favor of a law which
would permit us to purchase them and sail
them under the American flag, apparently ob-
livious to the fact that the steamers could not
be run in opposition to those of Great Britain
without the subsidies which had caused the success of the latter.

Notwithstanding the surplus of steam merchant vessels in Great Britain, the building of
iron and steel ships went on, while very few
were constructed on this side of the ocean. The
following table will show the effect of Government aid to British ocean steamers:

	Steamers
IRON VESSELS BUILT.	
1880, registered......................................	406
1881, registered......................................	465
1882, registered......................................	548
1883, registered......................................	678
1884, registered......................................	587

We can hardly realize in this country such a
wonderful activity in shipbuilding. There must
be powerful inducements to continue shipbuilding, even with a surplus of vessels on hand.
The purchase by Americans of their superfluous
ships was expected in England to open a still
more lively competition in the shipbuilding
industry, the English knowing that every vessel sold by them would be finally laid up in this
country, and would be so much steam tonnage
out of their way. "Free ships" would have
brought disaster on those who purchased them,
and all those industries connected with iron
shipbuilding in the United States would have
been destroyed.

To enumerate all the instances where the

British lines of steamers have been made suc
cessful through Government subsidies would
occupy too much space. I will confine myself
to the most important cases:

Details of the agreement entered into between the
British Admiralty and the owners of the White Star and
Cunard Companies, by which certain of their vessels are
placed at the disposal of the Government on specified
terms, are contained in a late parliamentary paper. The
White Star Line agrees to hold at the disposition of the
Government for purchase or hire, at the option of the
Admiralty, to be exercised from time to time during the
continuance of the agreement, the following vessels:
Britannic, value £130,000; Germanic, £130,000; Adri-
atic, £100,000; Celtic, £100,000. In the event of purchase the foregoing prices were to be held as the values
on the 1st of January, 1887, plus 10 per cent. for com-
pulsory sale, less an abatement of 6 per cent. per annum
on the depreciated annual value for the period that
might elapse between the 1st of January, 1887, and the
date of purchase by the Government. In the event of
charter by the Admiralty, the rate of hire of the before-
mentioned vessels was fixed at the rate of 20s. per gross
registered ton per month, the owner providing the crew,
or at the rate of 15s. per gross registered ton per month,
the Admiralty finding the crew, all risks of capture and
of hostilities being assumed by the Admiralty. The
company has determined to build one or two vessels of
high speed and of such a type and speed as will render
them specially suitable for service as armed cruisers, and
in accordance with the plans and specifications submit-
ted and approved by the Admiralty. In consideration of
this the Admiralty will have to pay to the company an
annual subvention at the rate of 15s. per gross registered
ton per annum. On the 8th of February the Admiralty
accepted similar proposals made by the Cunard Line in
respect to the following vessels: Etruria, value £310,000;
Umbria, £301,000; Aurania, £240,000; Servia, £193,-
000; Gallia, £102,000; a subvention of 15s. per gross
registered ton per annum to be paid to the company on
account of the Etruria, Umbria and Aurania during the
continuance of the postal contract, and in the event of
the termination of that contract before these three ves

sels received five years' payment, the company to be entitled to receive for the balance a subvention at the rate of 20s., the five vessels being still held at the disposition of the Government. In the event of the Cunard Company building new vessels for the mail service, they will submit the plans to the Admiralty for approval.

The subvention will amount to about £6,500 for each of the new vessels of the White Star Line, so long as they carry the mails, or £8,500 should the mails be withdrawn. The annual charge for the retention of the Cunarders Etruria, Umbria and Aurania is stated at £5,400 each. The Admiralty announces that they are ready to make the same arrangements as with the White Star Company for the first ten steamers that may be offered by any of the British steamship companies.

Only such ships are subsidized as have been carefully constructed under naval supervision, and are fully qualified for the duty of commerce-destroyers, troop-ships, store-ships, etc.

Since writing the above I have learned that three Cunard steamers have been purchased by the Canadian Pacific Railroad Company to ply between Vancouver and Hong-Kong, and the first voyage will commence at once.

It has been the custom in this country to have vessels that were paid to carry the mails inspected by the post-office officials, but such an inspection would merely show whether the vessels were seaworthy, not that they were able to carry guns. There is an impression existing in the minds of those who have not paid much attention to the subject, that the ordinary merchant steamer can, in an emergency, be readily converted into an efficient vessel of war. During the civil war we used a great many of these converted vessels, and although they answered the purpose of blockading the Southern ports very well, yet in the only case where one of them encountered a fairly armed cruiser she went to the bottom in fifteen minutes. Out of all the vessels in the American steam lines, of which I have given a list, there is not one which could be converted into an efficient cruiser without undergoing extensive alterations.

The merchant vessels we employed in the late war generally carried light 32-pounders and howitzers, but in future wars the smallest piece of ordnance likely to be used, with the exception of machine and rapid-firing guns, would be the 6-inch rifle. Vessels as at present constructed in the mercantile marine could not long endure the concussion of the 6-inch rifle, and if the 6-inch rifle would break down their decks, how much more would they feel the 8-inch guns, of which it would be desirable to have one or two on board each commerce-destroyer. Hence the Navy should not rely on those steamers we have now employed on our coast, or even some of those in use on the open ocean.

VI.

FRENCH SUBSIDIES.

For many years France tried the policy of free ships and free raw material, but finding that by so doing she was sacrificing her own interests and supporting the iron manufacturers of England, a law was passed in 1881 by the French Assembly, which changed the aspect of affairs in the mercantile marine of that country. When the bounty law was enacted the total shipping of France amounted to 914,373 tons. During the first year after the adoption of the law 161 steam vessels, of 122,276 tons, and

1,050 sailing vessels, of 39,733 tons, were added to the mercantile marine. This is pretty good proof of the efficacy of a bounty law to build up shipping, although so large an annual increase in French commerce has not taken place since 1881, owing to the business stagnation and the fact there is now tonnage enough to carry on the trade.

The bounty allowed by the French Government is a liberal one, both to steam and sailing vessels. It amounts to 17½ per cent. on the total cost price of a steamer; thus on a vessel of 8,000 tons, costing $900,000, the bounty would be $157,500. No vessels of this country could compete against such a subsidy as that, and, therefore, it has never been attempted.

The same law repealed the act granting free entry to imported articles included in the building of ships, thus encouraging French industries. It also provides that for any modification or alteration of a ship whereby her tonnage is increased, bounty shall be paid on the increased tonnage. Besides the above, the owner of a steamship is allowed a compensation of eight francs per hundred kilograms of new boilers of French make, weighed without the pipes. A compensation is allowed for the burden laid on the mercantile marine employed in foreign commerce, for the recruiting of sailors for the navy by a navigation bounty, given for a period of ten years from the date of enactment. Bounties on steamships are increased 15 per cent. in cases where the plans of the vessel have been approved by the Government.

A comparison of the French carrying trade during four years will show the effect of the bounty law upon the shipping of France :

Tables showing the volume of trade in French vessels.

ARRIVALS.

Trade at French ports with:	1881. Number.	1881. Tons.	1882. Number.	1882. Tons.	1883. Number.	1883. Tons.	1884. Number.	1884. Tons.
French colonies.	1,437	990,160	1,439	1,024,375	1,569	1,080,989	1,383	1,010,577
Sea fisheries	456	54,212	504	58,939	585	64,664	623	72,575
European foreign countries.	7,291	2,111,209	6,792	1,933,971	6,792	2,049,925	5,536	1,990,605
Countries beyond Europe..	767	763,961	783	950,732	879	1,165,411	793	1,107,819
Total	9,951	3,919,662	9,568	4,023,017	9,759	4,410,939	8,430	4,181,576

CLEARANCES.

Trade at French ports with:	1881. Number.	1881. Tons.	1882. Number.	1882. Tons.	1883. Number.	1883. Tons.	1884. Number.	1884. Tons.
French colonies.	1,625	1,112,094	1,690	1,102,092	1,793	1,273,278	1,691	1,257,042
Sea fisheries...	333	42,198	499	57,104	549	57,744	600	65,617
European foreign countries.	5,297	1,319,209	4,933	1,369,113	5,059	1,536,700	4,445	1,502,716
Countries beyond Europe..	821	881,414	842	1,056,844	895	1,221,824	759	1,094,582
Total	8,126	3,354,915	7,964	3,585,153	8,296	4,089,636	7,495	3,919,257

These tables show the great increase of the
sea trade since 1880, under the French bounty

system, for under the fostering care of the Government French vessels already perform 35 per cent. of the carrying trade with foreign countries. It does not require much calculation to show what the result would be to the commercial marine of the United States by the operation of a similar law. The story is told in France. That country has relieved herself of the burden of employing the mechanics of foreign countries to construct her merchant ships. She has built up her private ship yards and consequently increased.her naval power—depending chiefly on her own industries to make her a great commercial nation in time of peace and to build up a most powerful navy in time o war.

A result of the French bounty law has been that fine line of 8,000-ton steamers running from Havre to New York, equal in every respect to the best British merchant vessels, and which would make admirable commerce destroyers. By the same law the French have built up that powerful fleet, the Messageries Maritimes, con·sisting of 61 vessels of 157,620 tons, many of which could be converted for national purposes in time of war.

SUBSIDIES BY OTHER POWERS.

Italy for some years tried free trade in ships, but at the expense of her shipbuilding establishments. The Italian Government pays now a subsidy of 8,000,000 francs to the Florio and Rubattino Line of steamers for carrying the mails. This line consists of ninety steamers of from 500 to 5,000 tons, which ply to ports of the Mediterranean, India and China. Since 1885 a new law, similar to that of France, has been enacted in Italy to encourage the Italians to build their own steamers.

Ten years ago Germany had but a small commercial marine, but she now owns 529 steamers, aggregating 601,975 tons. Most of this tonnage is in large vessels purchased abroad, but extensive subsidies have been allowed by the Government, under which the German steam lines have been extended to all parts of the world.

And so it will be found that it is owing to the subsidies granted by foreign governments that the great steam lines are enabled to hold their own in the thoroughfares of trade, while for the want of this assistance to American steamers, our flag is seldom seen in those thoroughfares, nor will it be until our countrymen realize the necessity of adopting the system in use abroad.

To show how the commercial marine of the United States has fallen behind the other properties of the country, I will quote some suggestive figures. During the last twenty-five years the value of the property has increased more than three-fold, from $16,000,000,000 to $50,-000,000,000, the population during the same time has nearly doubled, the manufacturing products trebled, the farm products doubled, and railroad mileage quadrupled.

In 1860 we had vessels to the extent of 2,496,804 tons in foreign trade. In 1856 there were built 306 ships and barks, 103 brigs, 394 schooners and 497 sloops, a total of 404,054 tons. Thirty years later, in 1886, we built 8 ships, 1 brig, 274 schooners and 191 sloops.

In 1856 our foreign commerce amounted to $591,000,000. In 1886 it was nearly three times that sum. In 1856 we carried most of our commerce in our own ships. Now it is carried in foreign ones.

When we built ships they were the staunchest and fastest in the world, and it is fair to suppose that if we could again compete with foreign countries we should exhibit as much enterprise in building steamers as we did formerly in building sailing ships. We build the most magnificent river steamers in the world. Why could we not build the best sea-going ones?

These remarks concerning the necessity of building up the United States steam commercial marine, without which we cannot be considered a strong naval power, might be extended indefinitely. I consider the whole matter more particularly from a naval standpoint, although there are a multitude of reasons for building up our ocean-carrying trade. Compare its present condition with the wonderful increase in our other industries since the civil war, and you will see that we have paid out to foreign shipowners at least $3,000,000,000, and, worse than that, have lost the prestige which was formerly our country's pride.

I hope you will excuse me for taking up your time with matters which may not appear purely naval, but this is so much a naval question that without the resurrection of our mercantile marine we cannot become a strong naval power. When our mercantile marine is once established on a sure basis there will be no difficulty in Americans enjoying their fair share of the carrying trade. Traffic will follow the flag, as it did in the days of old, when the stars and stripes floated at the mastheads of the finest ships in the world. The cry that we have no foreign trade because we are a manufacturing nation will no longer be heard, for our steamships will carry these same manufactures to the remotest parts of the earth.

But to attain this desired end certain facts must be kept in view. Great Britain pays for ocean mail service to her steamships, not to mention other aids, $3,500,000 annually. The United States paid last year for foreign mail service $327,000 — less than one-tenth the amount paid by Great Britain—and of that sum $278,717.41 went to foreign vessels, leaving but a little over $48,000 paid to Americans.

At this moment we are indebted to the Brazilian Government for aid to enable us to run a line of American steamships to Brazil, said government paying $88,000 annually to the steamship company for carrying the mails,while the United States offered $5,000! The Argentine Republic offered $100,000 annually to an American company to carry the mails, while the United States offered $3,000, and in consequence of the want of liberality on the part of the United States the line cannot be established.

These facts are significant and offer a full explanation of the causes why the United States make so poor a show of steamships upon the ocean. This deficiency will continue until our law-makers take a more liberal view of the situation.

AMERICAN SHIPPING.

FROM THE REPORT OF THE COMMISSIONER OF NAVIGATION.

Unless the American ship in foreign ports, or in our own, can take cargoes as cheaply or more cheaply than the English, Norwegian, German or Spanish vessel, the merchandise will be transported by the foreign vessels. It is impossible without a change of the present conditions for our navigation to regain our lost supremacy in the foreign trade. Our vessels must be put on an equality with foreign ships, or they must be gradually forced out of the contest. Bounties or subsidies are paid by Spain, Italy, Germany, France, etc., and British vessels have been and are aided under one guise or another. The West Indian and South American trade, which naturally belongs to this country, is almost monopolized by European ships.

With regard to the coasting trade the case is different, and the shipping employed, amounting to 3,090,282 tons, without including many craft not documented, is reasonably prosperous, especially upon the lakes, where the coastwise trade is developing rapidly, the increase in the American tonnage there during the year ended June 30, 1887, being 21,161 tons. The gain upon the Pacific coast was 8,761 tons, and it was about the same on the Western rivers. The total documented tonnage of the United States is 4,105,844 tons, it being distributed as follows: Atlantic and Gulf, 2,638,272; Pacific

coast, 356,445; Northern lakes, 783,721; West
ern rivers, 328,405. The foreign going regis
tered tonnage is 1,015,562 tons.

I deprecate the many hardships encountered
by ship owners by reason of the constant change
going on in navigation from sail to steam, from
wood to iron and from iron to steel, and also by
reason of foreign bounties, subsidies and aids
granted to foreign ships competing with our
vessels, both in the merchant service and the
fisheries; that the Canadians should have made
the $5,500,000 foolishly given them by the
United States for almost worthless fishing privi-
leges, a fund, the interest on which is paid as a
bounty to Canadian fishermen competing with
our fishermen, who were already at a disadvan-
tage, on account of greater expense for vessels,
outfits, bait and wages. This condition of
affairs is in disobedience of the Bible injunction
not to seethe the kid in its mother's milk.